So, what's it like to be a cat?

Atheneum Books for Young Readers

An imprint of Simon & Schuster Children's

Publishing Division

1230 Avenue of the Americas

New York, New York 10020

Text copyright © 2005 by Karla Kuskin

Illustrations copyright © 2005

by Betsy Lewin

Book design by Ann Bobco

The text for this book is set in Priska and Evon.

The illustrations for this book are

rendered in watercolor.

Manufactured in China

First Edition

10 9 8 7 6 5 4 3 2

Library of Congress Cataloging-in-Publication Data

Kuskin, Karla.

So, what's it like to be a cat? / Karla Kuskin ;

illustrated by Betsy Lewin.—1st ed.

p.   cm.

Summary: A cat answers a young child's questions

about such things as how much and where it sleeps,

and whether or not it likes living with people.

ISBN 0-689-84733-5

[1. Cats—Fiction. 2. Stories in rhyme.] I. Lewin,

Betsy, ill. II. Title.

PZ8 .3.K96Wh 2005

[E]—dc22   2003027338

*This book is for Ian Swann Bell and his
cats, and his cousins and their cats, and his
oldest cousin, Jake, whose cats are dogs.*
—K. K.

To Slicky
—B. L.

So, what's it like to be a cat?

by
karla kuskin

illustrated by
betsy lewin

Atheneum Books for Young Readers
New York London Toronto Sydney

So, what's it like to be a cat?

I'm very glad you asked me that.

The day begins, for cats like me,
as all the world sleeps quietly.

I wake up in the friendly dark
long, long before the sun is bright.
It is the middle of the night,

and slipping out on silent feet,
I search for something nice to eat.

The hall is dark, your dish is too.
I'd be afraid if I were you.
The dark hides lots of scary stuff . . .

Dear Questioner, I've heard enough.
The hall *is* dark.
That's very true.
But I can see as well as you
when lights are on.

So I will eat till I feel fed,
then tiptoe softly back to bed.

Do you have a kitty bed
with your picture at the head?

I do *not* have a kitty bed
to rest my kitty tail and head.
I'd rather
sleep most anywhere
that's warm and soft:

a couch,

a chair,

a sleeping loft;
I'll curl up there.

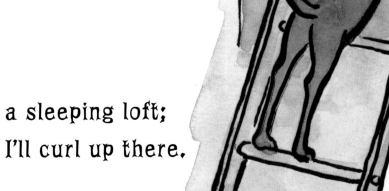

And once you're curled
you will not stir,
but nap
compactly wrapped in fur?

Meow. And how.

When they all get up for breakfast
in your early morning house,
do you sleep
or will you join them
for some breakfast Bits O' Mouse?

A cat has her habits.
A human has his.
As for "getting up for breakfast,"
I do not know what "breakfast" is.

My dog is always glad to see me.
He barks "good day"
and shares his bone.

But cats are private creatures
who are happier when left alone.
Of course I trust
and also wish
no one forgets to fill my dish
(a bit of fish might be delish).

I understand you sleep a lot,
but once in a while . . .

Cats have moods
like many creatures:
mothers, fathers, tigers, teachers.

So when I feel the need to prance
I run and whisk my tail
and dance.

And do you roar?
Please tell me more . . . .

To "do you roar?"
I have this answer—
I am a very silent dancer.
I whip through doors
and slip through alleys.

Bounce and pounce
and slide and sally,
rush and run
and twirl and spring
at you,
my tail,
or anything.

I whisk my whiskers,
pound my paws . . .

... because that is a part of me.
Sometimes a feline
must fly free.

We know you live with people.

Ah yes . . . a few.

Do you like them?
Do they like you?

With my catlike dignity
it never has occurred to me
to wonder what they think of me.
At times they're dumb.
At times they're sweet.
They balance nicely on their feet.
I do not think that I could do
half as well
on merely two.

But can they nap as fast as you?

They cannot do what I can do.
They do not nap or leap or lie
as gracefully or well
as I.
They look peculiar with no fur.
They do not simply sit and purr,
instead they stomp around and yell.

But nonetheless I wish them well.
They are themselves
and that is that.
Myself?

I'd rather be a cat.